I ♥ UNICORNS

Have fun completing the magical
activities in this book!

•

Use your pencils to color, doodle, and complete
the sparkly activities on each page.

•

You can use your puffy stickers in the book,
to finish your press-out pieces, or anywhere else
you want! Once you've removed the stickers,
you can use the cover as a frame
to display your favorite pictures.

make
believe
ideas

How to use your press-out pieces:

At the back of the book there are fun press-outs for you to decorate, display, or give away.

1 Pull out the card pages at the back of the book.

Pretty post
Press out and complete the cards, and then give them to your friends.

Dreamy door hanger
Press out the hanger, and then decorate it with your puffy stickers.

This room belongs to
....

2 Gently push the shapes until they pop out.

3 Complete the press-out pieces using color and your puffy stickers.

Perfect palace

Color
the palace.

Circle the unicorn that is different.

Dazzling diamonds

Find and circle the diamond that looks like this one.

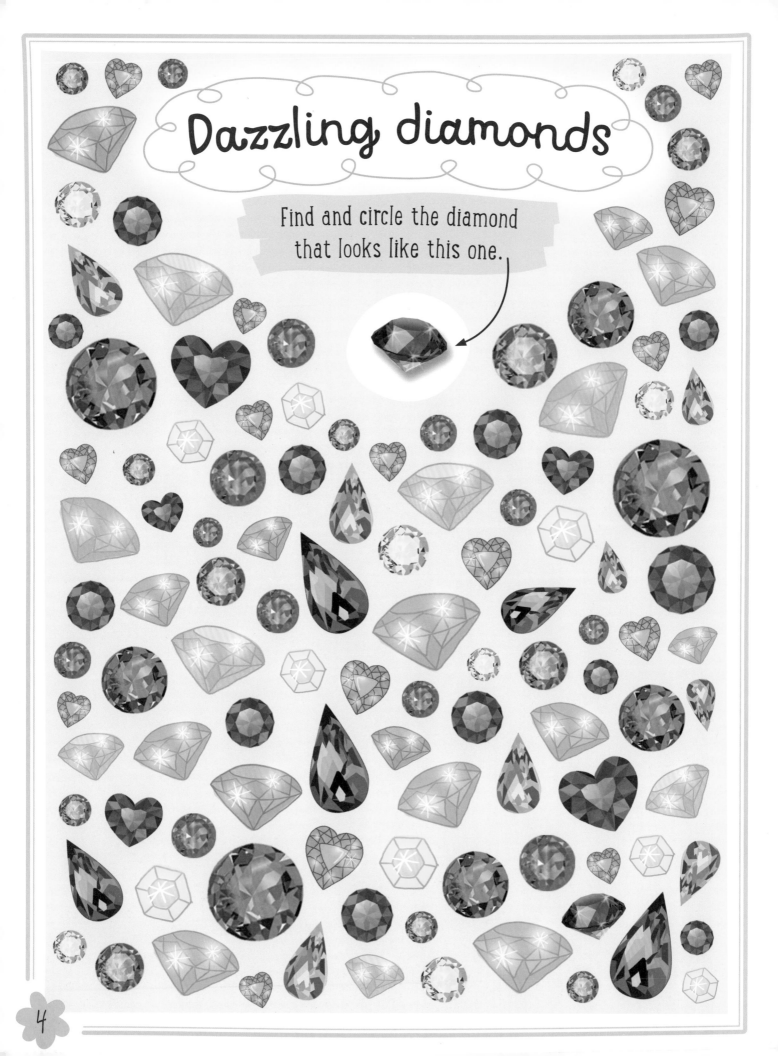

Unique unicorns

Circle five differences
between the two scenes.

Pretty patterns

Use colors to complete the pretty patterns.

Toadstool trot

Guide Ruby through the forest.
You can only jump on the toadstools.

Start

Finish

Fantasy Land

Search for the items below.
Check them off when you find them.

☐ 3 doves

☐ 4 orange flowers

☐ 5 fairies

☐ 4 unicorns

☐ 3 ducks

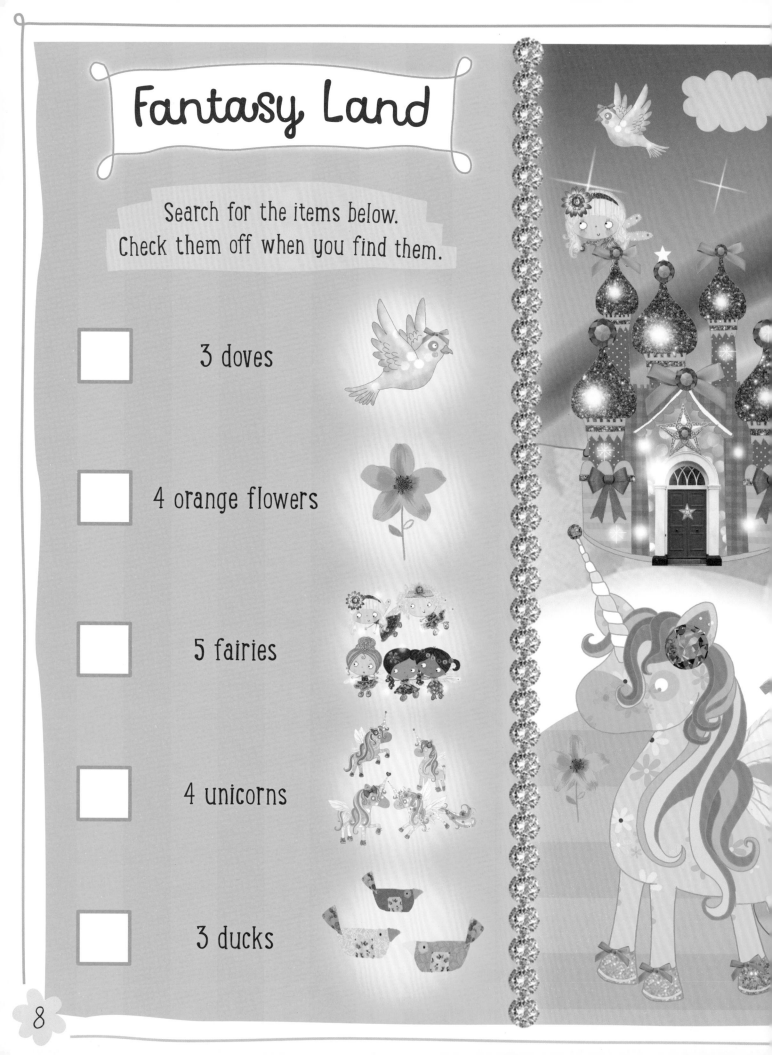

Sparkly search

Help Sparkle the unicorn find the words.
Words can go down or across.

```
b  f  s  t  a  r  s  q  j
j  w  r  o  f  j  l  h  s
e  t  k  o  y  h  e  y  p
w  o  c  r  o  w  n  k  a
e  b  z  s  c  t  g  n  r
l  p  l  f  a  e  t  p  k
t  v  g  d  r  p  q  r  l
z  u  n  i  c  o  r  n  e
```

crown

jewel

sparkle

stars

unicorn

Color match

Draw lines to link the unicorns with the matching colored horseshoes.

How many flowers can you see on the ground? ....

Wonderful wands

Trace the dots to finish the beautiful wands, and then add color.

Color
the gems.

Super spelling

Trace the letters to spell out the words.

wings

star

flower

magic

Dreamy jewelry

Use the key to color the scene.

1 = pink 2 = purple 3 = yellow
4 = blue 5 = orange 6 = red

15

Waterfall wander

Follow the lines to see which unicorn is going to the waterfall.

Fluttery friends

Use the clues to find out which unicorn
is Susie the fairy's best friend.

Susie

Sparkle

Stardust

Happy

Amber

Blueberry

Dandelion

CLUE 1:
The unicorn has
bows on her hooves.

CLUE 2:
The unicorn has a
white and pink horn.

CLUE 3:
The unicorn has
orange in her mane.

Which unicorn is Susie's best friend? ....

Tasty treats

The unicorns are baking!
Color the cupcakes and sweet treats.

Lovely letters

Unscramble the words below.
Use the pictures as a guide.

o r w c n

_ _ _ _ _

l e j w e

_ _ _ _ _

a c l t s e

_ _ _ _ _ _

w n d a

_ _ _ _

Picture perfect

Trace the lines to see who is in the enchanted garden.
Then add color and draw a face!

Color
the flowers.

Beautiful Bows

Find and circle the bow
that looks exactly like this one.

Copy the bow. Use the grid to help you.

Star maze

Guide Blueberry the unicorn through the star-shaped maze to reach her friend.

Start

Finish

How many red stars can you count? ......

Sparkly party

Add color to finish
the unicorn's party scene.

How many fairies can you see? ......

Sweet dreams

Draw what you think Happy the unicorn is dreaming about.

Wonderful words

Help Ruby the unicorn find the words.
Words can go down or across.

a	r	a	i	n	b	o	w	x	g
i	p	h	c	a	s	t	l	e	h
o	l	w	u	s	r	d	z	t	z
q	r	a	p	e	g	c	s	m	k
e	h	u	c	r	h	g	p	b	l
l	e	b	a	g	v	h	l	c	z
u	w	h	k	h	w	i	n	g	s
p	a	z	e	j	r	j	g	a	r
z	n	v	k	k	h	k	d	t	e
n	d	m	l	p	s	l	a	f	w

castle

cupcake

rainbow

wand

wings

25

What's different?

Circle the thing that is different in each group.

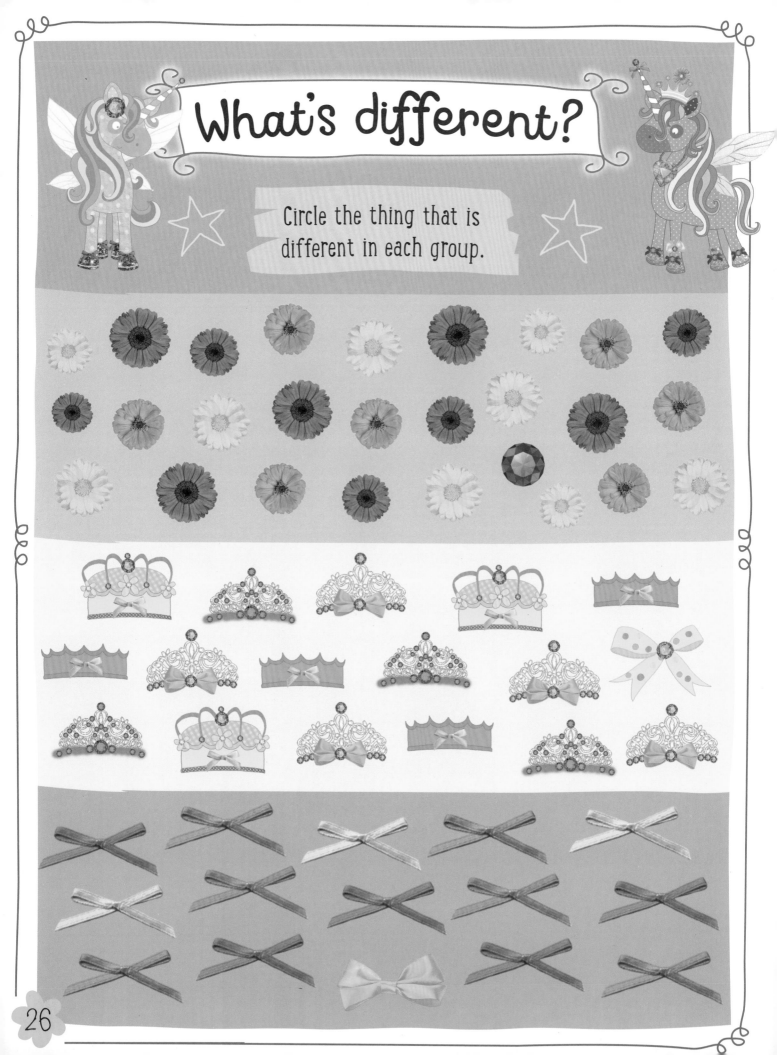

Rainbow weather

The unicorns are playing in the rain!

Draw faces on the cotton candy clouds.

Color the umbrellas.

Use your pencils to create rainbow-colored raindrops.

Flower fun

Use your pencils to complete the floral scene.

How many toadstools can you see?

....

Find the crown

Find and circle Amber the unicorn's crown.

29

Pretty pairs

Draw lines to match the pairs.

Shimmering sketches

Color and decorate the unicorns' wings.

Castle in the clouds

Connect the dots to complete the castle.
Then color it in!

Magical math

Help Stardust the unicorn count the flowers.

2 + 2 = 4

1 + 3 =

4 + 2 =

3 + 4 =

Fabulous frames

Color the pictures in the frames.

Give the unicorns colorful manes!

Draw a magical rainbow
in this frame.

Radiant rainbows

Color the rainbows and cotton candy clouds.
Use the colored dots as a guide.

Fantastic feasts

Amber is cooking up a fantastic feast.

Circle the one that doesn't belong.

Color the lollipops.

Draw toppings on the delicious cupcake.

Trace the dotted lines to copy the ice-cream cones.

Time to trace

Trace the letters to complete the words.

Color the enchanted garden scene.

Start →

s t a r s

p i c n i c

s p a r k l e

c a s t l e

Castle counting

Count the objects in each section.
How many can you see?
Write the answers in the boxes.

Crowns

....

Gems

....

Wands

....

39

Party planning

Help the unicorns get ready for a party.

Color Stardust's mane.

Trace and draw a pretty pattern on her wings.

Circle an orange bow, crown, and necklace for Amber to wear.

41

Cotton candy clouds

Stardust is flying through the clouds.
Draw a line from start to finish.

Start →

Visit all the
clouds and rainbows
along the way.

Avoid the
shooting stars!

→ Finish

Shiny sequences

Use colors to complete the shiny sequences.

Colorful coach

Connect the dots to complete the picture, and then color it.

Which way?

Use the key to draw a line from start to finish. Avoid the toadstools!

Key:

Start

Finish

45

Rainbow race

Help the unicorns reach the finish line!

Trace the trails!

Start →

Color the stars and jewels
for the unicorns to jump over.

Finish →

Prize-giving

Sparkle won the race!

Use the dots as a guide to color the rainbow.

Color the winner's cupcakes and add lots of yummy toppings.

Jewel Forest

Blueberry is trotting through the Jewel Forest.

Color Blueberry.

Look at the picture and check the boxes when you find things on the list.

- [ ] 4 toadstools
- [ ] 5 pink jewels
- [ ] 3 cupcakes

How many birds can you see?

....

Color the pretty petals on these flowers.

Tangled treats

Follow the lines to match the unicorns to their favorite foods.

Stardust

Amber

Dandelion

Sparkle stars

Trace the dots to create patterns in the night sky.

Use color to complete the scene.

Picture puzzle

Find and circle three purple things.

st_r

wa_d

_rown

Write the missing letters to finish the words.

Find the difference

Circle five differences between the two scenes.

Perfect pairs

Match the halves to make each unicorn's name.
You can find them all on page 17.

SPAR

DANDE

AM

HAP

STAR

BLUE

BER

BERRY

PY

LION

KLE

DUST

The first one has been done for you!

Yummy cupcakes

Help Blueberry color the cupcake.
Don't forget to add lots of tasty toppings!

How many berries
can you see?

Palace picnic

The unicorns are having a picnic.

Decorate the bunting.

Color the flowers.

56

Trace the lines and
color the candy clouds.

How many lollipops
can you count?

....

Color Dandelion.

57

Friends forever

Stardust is lost in the maze!
Can you help her find her friends?

Visit all the jewels, and don't go past any toadstools.

Finish

Start

Terrific tiaras

Find and circle the tiara that looks exactly like this one.

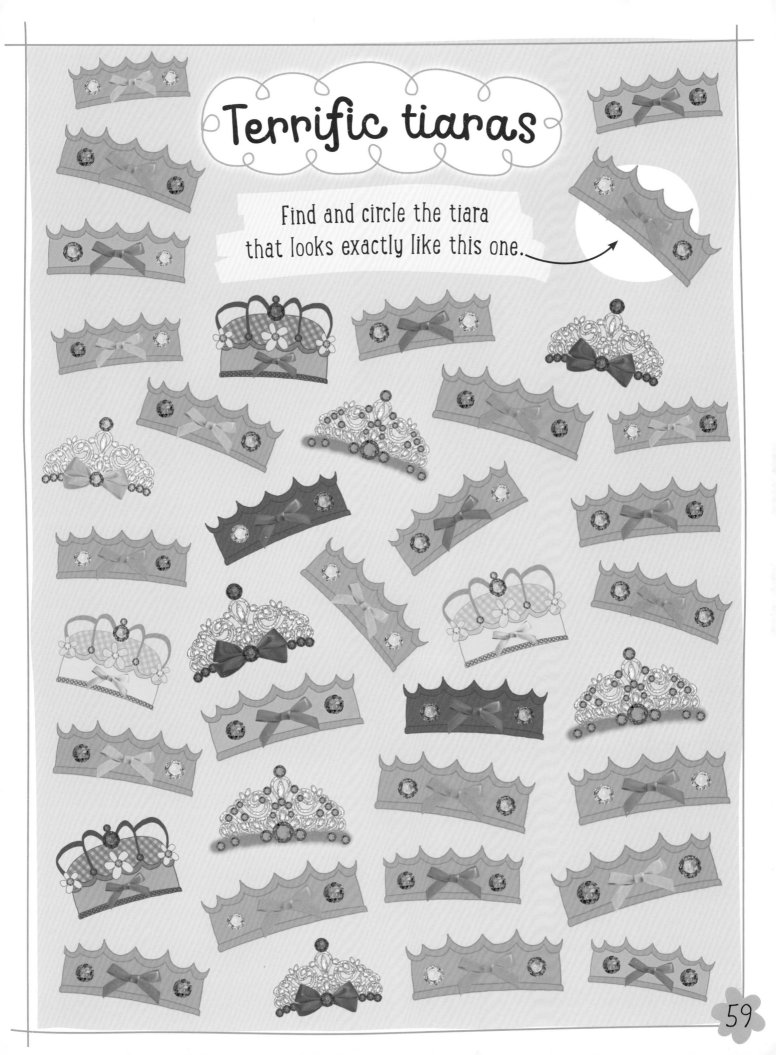

Time to trace

Trace the letters to reveal the words.

cloud

wand

fairies

rainbow

Unicorn quiz

Look at the rows of unicorns and find the ones that are different.

Who has a crown?	Who has a purple jewel on their ear?	Who wears an orange bow?	Who has gold hooves?
....	....	....	....

Write the correct number in the circles.

Rainbow maze

Guide Blueberry through the maze to reach the end of the rainbow.

Start

Finish

Sparkle splash

Use your pencils to color the water droplets in rainbow colors.

Color Amber.

Circle two purple ducks.

Color by numbers

Use the key to color the picture.

1 = red
2 = blue
3 = pink
4 = purple
5 = yellow

64

Magic models

These four pages contain the press-out pieces for you to make your very own magical land of fairy-tale unicorns! Press out the shapes and shade the reverse sides. Then, prop up the pieces using the stands.

Magic models

Press out the unicorn shapes and shade the reverse sides.
Then, prop up the pieces using the stands.

Glitter gardens

Press out the garden shapes and shade the reverse sides.
Then, fold the pieces to make them stand up.

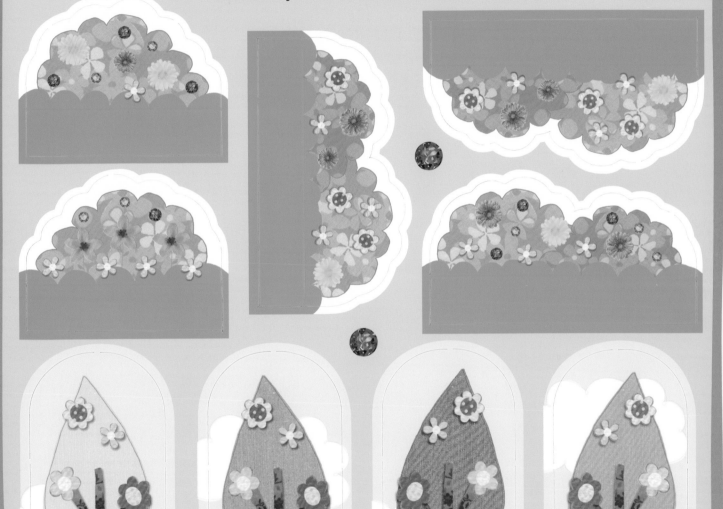

Sparkle scenes

Press out the waterfall scene, and then prop up the pieces using the stands.

Brilliant bunting

Press out each flag and ask an adult to help you fold the tops over some ribbon. Tape them down at the back, and then hang them wherever you want to make brilliant bunting!

Dreamy door hanger

Press out the hanger, and then
decorate it with your puffy stickers.

This room belongs to

....

Pretty post

Press out and complete the cards, and then give them to your friends.

Beautiful bookmarks

Press out these beautiful bookmarks and keep a record of the books you've read on the back!

Perfect pairs

This is a game for 1 to 2 players.

Instructions:

1. Press out the cards, and arrange them picture-side down on a table.

2. Take turns turning over two cards. If the cards match, put them aside. If they do not match, return them picture-side down to the table.

3. Keep going until you have found all the pairs. The winner is the player with the most pairs at the end.